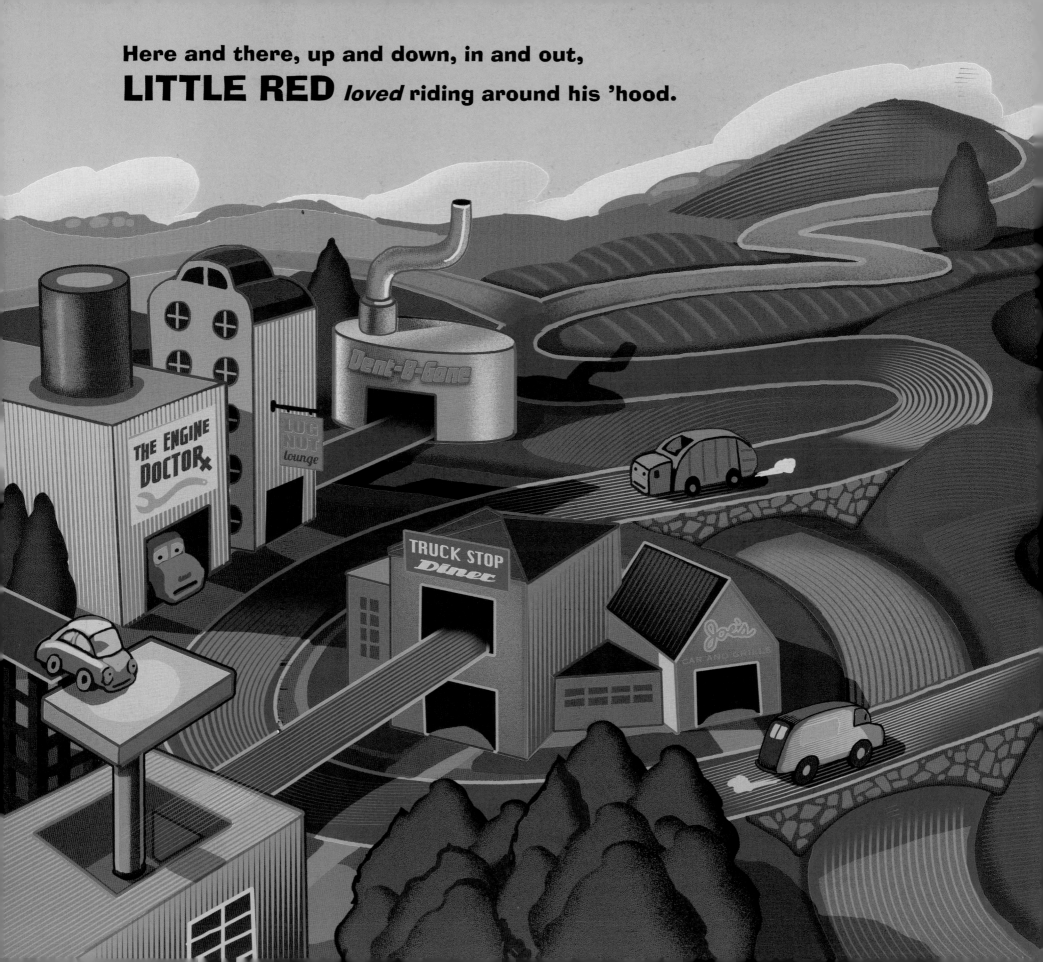

Here and there, up and down, in and out,
LITTLE RED *loved* riding around his 'hood.

One day, Big Blue Mama gave Little Red an important job.

"Poor Granny Putt Putt is feeling run-down," she said. "Her oil is muddy, her exhaust pipe's exhausted, and her wiper fluid is wiped out. Please take her this basket of goodies right away."

Little Red was excited — and a little nervous.

He'd never ridden all the way to Granny's house by himself.

Zipping to the top of Too Tall Hill, Little Red heard a familiar sound.
There sat Tank, King of the Road.

"**Yo, Red**," purred Tank. "Whatcha doin' way out here?"

"Granny Putt Putt's feeling run-down," squeaked
Little Red. "I'm taking her a special delivery."

"Well, burn my rubber!" said Tank. "That oil's too thin and those plugs won't spark! Head over to Zip's Auto Bonanza and tell 'em Tank sent you. They've got the goods to make Granny feel **showroom-new!**"

Little Red's caution lights flashed. Tank was usually one mean machine — why was he being so nice?

But Red wanted the very *best* for Granny Putt Putt. "She'll be SO excited!" he buzzed.

"HA!" cranked Tank, as mean and hungry as ever. "Now it's off to Granny's for some goodies of my own!"

VROOM!
DIDI-
DIDI-
DIDI

The monster truck took a shortcut to Granny's garage, blasted in, and swallowed her **WHOLE!**

With a big, satisfied burp, Tank climbed into Granny's bed, disguising himself with a frilly car cover and windshield glasses.

"Now it's time for some sweet **scooter dessert!**"

He didn't have to wait long.

"**Beep-beep!** Hi, Granny Putt Putt!
It's Little Red with a special delivery!"

"Oh, DO come in, my precious Little Red," cackled Tank

in his best Granny voice.

Little Red idled into the room. Something felt out of alignment.

"Why, Granny, what big **wheels** you have," said Little Red.

"All the better to cruise with you, my little scooter," creaked Tank.

"Why, Granny, what big **headlights** you have," said Little Red.

"All the better to shine on you, my little scooter," squeaked Tank.

"Why, Granny!" exclaimed Little Red.
"What a big *GRILLE* you have!"

"ALL THE BETTER TO *EAT* YOU WITH, SCOOTER BOY!" roared Tank.

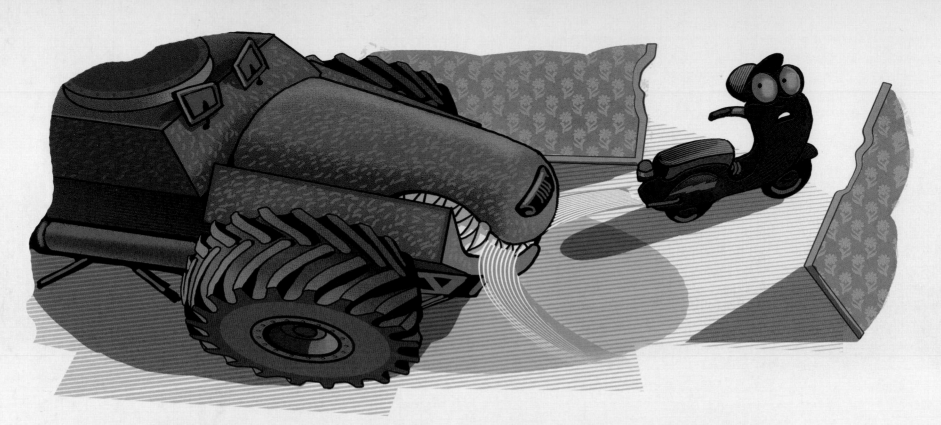

But Red was too quick for that big, bad monster truck.

He zipped out the door, down the driveway, and up the street.

Tank **cranked** it into high gear, black smoke billowing from behind.

"Come back here," he honked, "you puny little piston!"

They hit *top speed* over Too Tall Hill as Tank inched closer ... and closer ... **and closer!**

But now they'd reached Little Red's riding 'hood,
which Red knew like the back of his handlebars.

With Tank about to **CRUNCH** down on his rear bumper,
Little Red cranked a super-tight right turn!

That monster of a machine rocketed forward,

jumped the guardrail, and barreled through the air . . .

. . . crashing headlong into Jumbo Jim's Junkyard!

Tank's huge hood flew open and out popped Granny —
a bit greasy and dazed, but in fine working order.

Once all the dust settled, Granny thanked Little Red
for being the bravest scooter in town.

And Tank? Well, that crash cooled his engines for good.

He spent the rest of his days directing traffic . . .

for the NEW King of the Road...
Little Red!